Conger Rand

Jack Mason

Copyright © 2024 Jack Mason

All rights reserved.

No part of this publication may be reproduced, distributed, or transmitted in any form or by any means, including photocopying, recording, or other electronic or mechanical methods, without the prior written permission of the publisher, except in the case of brief quotations embodied in reviews and certain other non-commercial uses permitted by copyright law.

Dedication

For my brother Tim - my constant companion on innumerable adventures of imagination in childhood.

P1

So you seek the Conger Rand,
Exotic beast of far-flung land,

It's a long way to travel,
You'll need a crew,

It surely will be an adventure for you.

P2

The Conger Rand is rarely seen,
All we have really is folklore, I mean,

When you mention the beast,
You will feel sad, longing,

That comes from your wistful need for belonging.

P3

There's only been a few sightings reported,
And we cannot know if that numbers contorted,

It's mostly just feelings,
That draws men to roam,

To seek out the beast so far from one's home.

P4

In fables of the Conger Rand,
It's said, "Don't let it touch your hand,"

It dazzles your senses,
They note a red spark,

There's tale of it pulling you down in the dark.

P5

The Conger Rand lives in grasslands, they say,
And it cannot be found in the light of day,

To have a chance of success,
On this mission,

We'll need to mount a small expedition.

P6

We'll have cross oceans and forests and more,
We'll need to find people to help us explore.

We'll need to hire soldiers,
And workers and cooks,

We'll need a good guide, and we'll need balanced books.

P7

The Conger Rand is both man and dog,
It's painfully thin, and it hunts in the fog,

It walks on two legs,
Its fur is quite mottled,

There are legends of the explorers, it's throttled.

P8

The expedition will need to be up to the task,
The men will have orders to do what we ask.

Some of the expedition,
May die,

It's worth the cost - we have to try.

P9

We have to find the Conger Rand,
We have to sate the need at hand,

There's a powerful pull,
Calling us overseas,

It's a life-or-death call and can be felt in the breeze.

P10

We'll hire the men and buy the supplies,
We'll contract a ship to get us to the prize.

We'll leave in three days.
On the ship, that's on station,

We'll leave to our fates at our destination.

P11

Let's say our goodbyes before we depart,

And speak to our loved ones once more from the heart,

Then, we must move on,

And leave them behind,

And only have our adventure in mind.

P12

The day to leave has finally arrived,
The moment is here for which we have strived,

Load up the ship with the supplies,
And the men,

We will not be coming home again.

P13

Our ship has sailed for the land,
Where we may find the Conger Rand,

We're now committed.
As the beast, we pursue,

The ocean will be the first test for the crew.

P14

The ocean voyage has caused some strain,

On our patience and nerves, but it's worthwhile pain,

We're halfway there,

And we must bear more,

Another two weeks and we'll see the shore.

P15

We've sighted the beaches and palm trees and sand,
That looks like they match with our target land

Let's go to the small boats,
And let's disembark,

The expedition can make landfall by dark.

P16

We made landfall at a point on the beach,
Inland is next to the forest's great reach,

We'll camp here this evening,
And sleep here tonight.

We'll start trailblazing at morning's first light.

P17

We lost one of our soldiers last night,
He looked like he had died of fright.

He is the first,
Of our company to die,

But that is the cost of our crucial try.

P18

To find the forest is the next test,

It's a problem that has puzzled our best,

We don't exactly know,

The way that we should head,

But we can make a bearing of our inner dread.

P19

We're trailblazing out in force
Along that bearing for our course

From beaches to deserts,
To prairie expanse,

The fate of our journey resting on chance.

P20

And it seems like we're getting horribly lost,
The journey always exacting more cost,

We just lost two workers,
They seem to have bled,

Out from their ears, while lying in bed.

P21

After three days, we catch a reprieve,
Giving relief, that is hard to believe,

We've spotted the forest,
And its verdant border,

Can be reached by our men is fairly short order.

P22

We're closer to the Conger Rand,
But the next phase has to be planned,

We make camp,
In the green forest trees,

Treasuring moments of respite like these.

P23

Another worker dead in the night,
He simply expired- there was no fight!

He went to the woods,
For a short time,

And collapsed as he walked- cut down in his prime.

P24

It's time to draft the forest plan,

We have to take it, or we'll lose each man,

There's just one safe path,

We can take,

Ignoring the legends would be a mistake.

P25

According to the myths and lore,
This route we haven't seen before,

Winding out through the trees,
Like a metronome,

If we don't stick to it, we'll be lost as we roam.

P26

If the path isn't followed at any cost,
The legends say that we all will be lost,

There can be no shortcuts,
Despite the great distance,

Or the forest will wipe you out of existence.

P27

Our guide found the path - it's not far away,
Let's break down the camp and move out today,

The path is faded, and,
Broken and thin,

We'll go single file as we journey in.

P28

Closer to the Conger Rand,

Traipsing through woods in a far-off land,

The call is still heard,

It's pulling on you.

It's worth any of the lives of the crew.

P29

The forest path is rocky and grey,
Weathered and worn in that time-aged way,

Our company filters through,
One by one,

On the road to the prize, til the mission is done.

P30

Along the path are seas of trees,
We've never seen them quite like these,

They're gnarled and old,
They're withered and grey,

The trees make you want to go astray.

P31

We walk for days inside the wood,
With no way to know if our progress is good,

It shouldn't be hard,
It's a simple endeavor,

Stick to the path or be lost forever.

P32

The sea of trees fills your view as you trudge,
It overwhelms you that the trees will not budge,

Calm is replaced,
As we walk on the path,

Instead of calm reason, it fills you with wrath.

P33

The path is unceasing as we journey on,
Our patience, and hope, and grace are all gone,

As the forest grey spores,
And mists fill the air,

Our men start going quite mad with despair.

P34

We've lost more men on the path as we've traveled,

As functioning people, we've simply unraveled,

Some have jumped off the path,

We'll soon have a count,

Some have fallen to wraiths in equal amount.

P35

We lost key men getting to this position,
But's there still enough to achieve our mission,

The loss should be sad,
The expedition is bruised,

But all of those men were meant to be used.

P36

The path ahead seems to curve on a bend,
Something is different- can this be the end?

Though the path through the forest,
Brought us to our knees,

We can see space and light through the trees.

P37

We send a scout through to the other side,
He came back at nightfall with news to provide,

We're now at the grasslands,
This trial is done,

And finding the beast might be the last one.

P38

Searching for the Conger Rand,

It should be in this grassland,

We've crossed the world,

To get where we are,

The lives lost were worth it to make it this far.

P39

We've set up our camp since we need to rest,
Our guide suggested that it would be best,

Just one more night,
And we can resume,

The hunt for the beast and its projected gloom.

P40

The final leg of our journey can start,
Adventure borne of gloom and of heart,

Our numbers have dwindled,
But success is in sight,

All we need to do from here is hold tight.

P41

The grasslands sweep out like a golden sea,
We do not know what our next step will be,

Our guide found a high bluff,
Out in the distance,

We'll go there to make the best choice in this instance.

P42

We climbed up the bluff and looked out on the land,
Surveying ahead from up on the stand,

There's a river ahead,
Almost out of view,

That will be the next landmark we go to.

P43

The river is a two-day march from the bluff,
The terrain's mostly flat and doesn't look rough,

Though it's just a guess,
The call is now strong,

One feels we might find the beast before long.

P44

We've walked one day on our course that we marked,
It's been easygoing as our people embarked,

There's been no movement,
That we have yet seen,

The landscape approach is both calm and serene.

P45

It is day two of our course to the river,
The temperature's cooled, causing us a light shiver,

We can smell water,
And the grasslands abound,

The beauty around us all is profound.

P46

We set up camp in the grasslands tonight,

Tomorrow, the river should be within sight,

We will stay here this evening,

And let the men rest,

Tomorrow will be our crucible test.

P47

There's cheer in the air as the men now unwind,
There's excitement and wonder about what we will find,

There's a smell in the breeze,
It smells like a bog,

And slowly the land begins twisting with fog.

P48

The fog's white and thick and curls like a snake,
It curls at your feet and makes your body ache,

The night is so dark,
Our cheer turns to ash,

There's a scream in the night before a red flash.

P49

The men strain their eyes to see it's coming,
The fog is now thick and is cold and is numbing,

They mount a defense,
As the fog makes them cough,

Their screams fill the night as a form picks them off.

P50

It pulls the men down one by one in the mist,

Some try to escape, but none can resist,

It moves like a beast,

Like a man or a dog,

There are also red sparks flashing bright in the fog.

P51

The last of our soldiers are dead in the mist,
Our guide was cut down as he tried to assist,

There's only a few workers,
Left in the night,

There's the odd scream and the odd flash of red light.

P52

With one last scream fading into the fog,

You see a thin beast- part man and part dog,

The Conger Rand,

Picked off your whole crew,

And now it's surely coming for you.

P53

You feel like you're floating- you don't understand,

You see a red light sparking up from it's hand,

You're feeling so tired,

You just need some rest,

There's a brush on your hand and bile in your chest.

P54

If you meet the Conger Rand,
Do not let it touch your hand,

It will dazzle your senses,
You'll see a red spark,

And then it will pull you down in the dark.

P55

Now you've met the Conger Rand,
Did the beast just brush your hand?

You look in its eyes,
They're filled with cold gloom,

A sense of belonging then starts to bloom.

P56

So you met the Conger Rand,

It paralyzed you, and it touched your hand,

And you were pulled down,

Into the dark,

Now, it's your hand giving off a red spark.

P57

You had to seek the Conger Rand,
And now, your end is here at hand,

You feel horrid change,
But now it's too late,

Now, you, in turn, pull them down to their fate.

www.ingramcontent.com/pod-product-compliance
Lightning Source LLC
LaVergne TN
LVHW012037060526
838201LV00061B/4650